tle Miss Muffet's Big Scare

First published in 2009
by Wayland

This paperback edition published in 2010

Wayland
338 Euston Road
London NW1 3BH

Wayland Australia
Hachette Children's Books
Level 17/207 Kent Street
Sydney, NSW 2000

Series Editor: Louise John
Editor: Katie Powell
Cover design: Paul Cherrill
Design: D.R.ink
Consultant: Shirley Bickler

A CIP catalogue record for this book is available from the British Library.

ISBN 9780750256025 (hbk)
ISBN 9780750258159 (pbk)

Printed in China

Wayland is a division of Hachette Children's Books,
an Hachette Livre UK company
www.hachettelivre.co.uk

Little Miss Muffet's Big Scare

Written by Alan Durant
Illustrated by Leah-Ellen Heming

WAYLAND

Little Miss Muffet was a girl with a curl in the middle of her forehead.

When she was bad she was very, very bad and when she was good... well, she was never good, she was always horrid.

She loved to sit on her tuffet and play nasty tricks on everyone. One day, Doctor Foster came and asked the way to Gloucester.

Little Miss Muffet said, "It's that way," and directed him into the biggest, deepest puddle you ever did see.

Poor Doctor Foster was in water right up to his middle!

One night, the man in the moon tumbled down on his way to shine on Norwich. Little Miss Muffet was sitting on her tuffet, eating from a bowl.

"That looks nice," said the man in the moon. "What is it?"
"It's cold pease-porridge," said Little Miss Muffet.

"Oooh!" exclaimed the man in the moon. "That's my favourite!"
"Try some," said Little Miss Muffet and, smiling, she handed him the bowl.

But the pease-porridge wasn't cold, it was so hot it burned the man in the moon's mouth. "Ow!" he yelled.

When Jack moaned that he'd fallen down a hill and cut his head, Little Miss Muffet told him to pour vinegar on his wound and wrap it in brown paper.

Well, of course all that did was make the cut sting even more and make Jack look very silly. Little Miss Muffet laughed and laughed.

The worst trick that Little Miss Muffet played was on Mrs Ladybird. She told her that her house was on fire and all her children had gone.

Poor Mrs Ladybird nearly had a heart attack — and, of course, it wasn't true.

What a wicked, wicked girl Little Miss Muffet was.

Finally, everyone had had enough. "It's time we taught that wicked girl a lesson," they said.

The first to try was Georgie Porgie.
"I'll kiss her," he said. "That'll make
her cry. Girls always do when I
kiss them."

But Little Miss Muffet didn't cry. She laughed and stuck out her tongue at Georgie Porgie, which made HIM cry.

"I'll scare her," said Pussy Cat, "just like I scared those mice under the queen's chair. I'm the fiercest cat there is."

She hissed and snarled at Little
Miss Muffet, but the bad little girl
just laughed.

Then she roared at Pussy Cat and
chased HER away.

"I know what to do with bad children,"
said the old woman who lived in a
shoe. "I've got lots of them. I'll give
her a good beating with my stick."

But Little Miss Muffet was too quick for the old woman. She grabbed the stick and beat her on the bottom. Then she broke the stick in two.

There was only one thing left to do. It was time to call for the scariest person of all, the man who gave everybody the shivers – Doctor Fell! Surely HE would scare Little Miss Muffet.

Doctor Fell went to see Little Miss Muffet. He stared at her with his beady eyes. He smiled his scary crooked grin. He opened his bag of nightmares and took out a black bottle.

"Try some of my lovely medicine,"
he croaked.
"Thanks," chirped Little Miss Muffet.

She took a big swig... then she spat
it out, right in Doctor Fell's face!
"I'm not scared of you," she laughed.

Little Miss Muffet sat on her tuffet, eating her favourite dish of curds and whey – and feeling very pleased with herself.

"I'm not scared of anything," she said.
But she was wrong.

Suddenly, out of a water spout next to her tuffet, an incey wincey spider appeared.

It crept over to Little Miss Muffet and sat down beside her.

Little Miss Muffet turned and...
"Agh! A spider!" she shrieked.

She jumped up and threw her bowl
in the air.

Then she ran away as fast as she could, screaming her head off.

And, from that day to this, she's never been seen again!

START READING is a series of highly enjoyable books for beginner readers. **The books have been carefully graded to match the Book Bands widely used in schools.** This enables readers to be sure they choose books that match their own reading ability.

Look out for the Band colour on the book in our Start Reading logo.

The Bands are:

Pink Band 1

Red Band 2

Yellow Band 3

Blue Band 4

Green Band 5

Orange Band 6

Turquoise Band 7

Purple Band 8

Gold Band 9

START READING books can be read independently or shared with an adult. They promote the enjoyment of reading through satisfying stories supported by fun illustrations.

Alan Durant has written many stories and poems for children of all ages. He loves nursery rhymes and often makes up his own like this one:
Hinky-hunky, hankily-dunky
I am a queen, and you are a monkey!

Leah-Ellen Heming once brought back a mouse from her studio in her backpack and cycled it all the way up a very steep hill to her house, where it escaped. The mouse then had a big family, but Leah caught them all and unleashed the mice in her friend's allotment, where they now live happily ever after.